PRIMITUS

FRANKIE JAMES

Book Cover by Christian Bentulan www.coversbychristian.com

Formatting by BookADayDay Formatting

Proofreading by Trisha Elaine

 Formatted with Vellum

CONTENTS

PROLOGUE

ADELAIDE

"That's it, baby. Just breathe through it." John squeezed my hand. "You're doing an amazing job."

"You're a goddess." Jesse squeezed my hand from the other side of the bed and brushed my hair back gently.

I smiled weakly, appreciating their encouraging words. However, it was probably more a gritting of teeth than a smile. I definitely didn't feel like a goddess. Sweat was trickling down my face, and my hair was in a messy bun that had slid to the side of my head above my left ear.

"Deep breath in...that's good, Adelaide. Now let it out slowly." Shannon, my doula, said in a soothing voice.

I'd gone to the nearest Aurathion town and interviewed several birthing experts. When I met Shannon, I knew she was the right fit immediately. She had such a calming presence about her, and I knew I would need that. My men were wonderful, but I couldn't count on them to hold their shit together while I was in labor.

"How much longer?" I gritted out.

"You're dilated to an eight. Things will move much quicker now." Shannon rose from her position at the end of the bed. "I'm going to get you a cup of crushed ice and give you three a moment alone."

"I don't think it's a good idea for you to leave." John frowned, clearly not a fan of the idea.

"My brother's right, what if the baby comes while you're downstairs?" Jesse had a look of complete panic on his face.

Shannon smiled, "Then you yell for me to come back up or send one of your critters to get me."

There were at least five animals in my room right now. They were all sensing John's distress and wanted to be close. When my labor first began, Moxie had used her little paws to rub my hair, trying to soothe me. She was a raccoon that had shown up not long after we moved in and hadn't left since.

"It's only the fucking kitchen, Jesse, not Aurathia." I gritted out as I felt another contraction coming on.

John winced at my language but knew better than to say anything in this moment.

I squeezed both of their hands tightly and tried to breathe through the pain like Shannon had taught me. The contractions were coming so quickly now that one was rolling into another with hardly any break in between.

Shannon used the distraction to leave the room quietly. She knew our story and all the sacrifices we'd made to be here. The last eight months had been horrible, and without this precious life I was bringing into the world, I don't know if I would've made it.

John kissed my hand, then hurried into our bathroom. He came back shortly and wiped the sweat from my forehead. The cool, damp rag felt wonderful on my heated skin.

I breathed through the last of the contraction, and tears came to my eyes. "I wish Sly and Rue were here."

I'd tried to stay strong and not mention them. I didn't want to upset John and Jesse, but I was in so much pain that it was impossible to shield my emotions. I longed so badly for them to be here to witness the birth of our child.

Jesse's eyes grew sad. "They would've given anything to be here with us, you know that."

"Please don't cry, baby girl," John leaned down and kissed me gently. "This baby is a little piece of each of us, and they would've sacrificed their life ten times over to make sure our child is safe."

"I know you're right, but I want them *here!*" I began to cry, stopping abruptly as the next contraction stole my breath.

The pain was excruciating. My stomach started to burn from the inside. I felt my Nexus mark begin to tingle. Then my face heated so quickly that the tears dried on my cheeks.

Something wasn't right.

"Get Shannon!" I screamed as another wave of intense pain hit me. Now the burning had consumed my entire body.

"I knew she shouldn't have left!" Jesse ran out of the room in panic, screaming Shannon's name.

John didn't leave my side, flinging the rag on the night-stand, the heat from my face rendering it useless.

"Baby, what's happening?" He sat down on the bed beside me, "Please Adelaide, tell me what to do."

My heart broke from the look of helplessness on his face; John was the one who usually had all the answers, so I knew this was killing him. I wanted to reassure him, but the pain was so intense that I wasn't able to speak.

None of this was normal.

I felt my body levitate slightly off the bed just as Shannon and John came rushing into the room. I was so hot at this point that I felt like my blood was boiling.

"Help her!" John pleaded.

The burning was turning into a cold that was beyond anything I'd ever felt. My teeth started to chatter, and I began shaking uncontrollably. Then the heat started back up, burning my insides once again.

"I've never seen anything like this. Some Aurathions will have abilities that act up during labor, but nothing like this. She's actually glowing." I could hear the amazement in her voice even through my pain.

"Stop staring and do something about it!" Jesses growled, losing control of his ability and partially shifting. Traces of his wolf evident in his voice.

Shannon squeaked, "Wet towels...that's what we need. It'll help bring her temp down. While you're doing that, I'll make some calls."

"No!" I screamed, startling everyone. "No one can know about this."

"Why?" Shannon asked, panic clear on her face.

My contraction ended, and the craziness paused for the moment.

"I don't know *why*, but I feel like it's important to keep this between us," I spoke through gritted teeth, narrowing my eyes at the woman in warning.

I couldn't explain it, but I knew if we told anyone it would end badly for us and our baby. Precognition wasn't one of my abilities, or at least not one I'd gained up to this point. I hadn't told my men, but since Rue and Sly's absence, I'd noticed my abilities becoming more and more unstable.

"I don't have any experience with this, and if you don't let me contact my colleagues, I'm not sure how much help I can be." Shannon shrugged her shoulders.

I could tell she disapproved, but I didn't give a damn. The safety of our baby was all that mattered. I'd do whatever it took to make sure this precious child was protected.

John and Jesse looked at me, then turned to look at each other, communicating in the special way only twins could. Sly used to get pissed at them for not including the rest of us in their mental conversations.

"Please, guys, you have to trust me," I begged telepathically.

Both of them nodded in unison, then turned their narrowed gazes toward Shannon. I'd seen many a man tremble when they received that look. My two men were beyond intimidating when they wanted to be.

John spoke, "It will be as our Nexus asks. If you disagree, you're welcome to leave."

Shannon rolled her eyes, seeming to be made of

stronger stuff than I expected. "Of course I'm not leaving. If Adelaide feels this strongly, then I'll do as she wishes."

At that precise moment, the pain came back along with the alternating sensations of burning and freezing. I wasn't sure how much longer I could handle this.

Suddenly, I felt intense pressure and knew it was time.

"I need to push." I panted, giving Shannon a pleading look.

She rushed to the end of the bed. "The baby is crowning. Okay, Adelaide, when the next contraction hits, you can start pushing."

I nodded my head and grimaced, the next contraction rolling over my body as soon as the last had receded. My men came to stand on either side of my bed and I was grateful for their support.

"You've got this Nexus...now push." Shannon gave me a reassuring smile of encouragement.

I held onto John and Jesse's hands, gritted my teeth, and pushed with all of my might.

It still felt strange to realize I was bringing a child into the world. I'd never pictured myself as a mother. When I met all of my wonderful men, none of us could have predicted the challenges we would face or how it would end.

My time at Emberhold Academy remains the best of my life, up to this point. It's wild to think it all began because of my shit roommate and my knack for always being late...

CHAPTER I

ADELAIDE

EMBERHOLD ACADEMY

"Could this day possibly get any worse?' I muttered to myself as I rushed into the main hall of Emberhold Academy. I knew that saying that out loud was tempting fate to prove that it, *in fact*, could get worse.

My day started perfectly, but it quickly went downhill. I'd slept well and got dressed with plenty of time to spare. (That's highly unusual for me.) Then someone delivered breakfast from Java and Jam to my dorm, my favorite place to eat on campus.

Unfortunately, that's where everything took a turn for the worse.

My roommate Selene was a bitch. There was no other way to put it. From the first day we met, she'd been a real piece of work, criticizing everything about me. I was too short, my hair was too pale, my eyes were too close together-blah, blah, blah. You name it, she had something shitty to say.

Lucky for me, I was a reasonably confident girl. Everything she said went in one ear and out the other. I knew the drill. Everyone here was super competitive and wanted to form the most powerful Faction.

Why some Aurathions thought you had to tear each other down to do it was beyond me. If you followed the ways of our ancestors, you knew there were certain people out there just for you—no need to step on each other to find them. We should be straightening each other's crowns, not trying to rip them off.

The less I responded to her, the worse she got. I'm sure other girls crumbled in the face of her bullshit, and when I didn't, her shitty behavior escalated.

This morning, she truly outdid herself.

⤳ ⚜ ⤵

*"*T*hose donuts are for me." Selene scowled as I walked back into the dorm.*

"That's odd because the card on the box clearly has my name on it." I tried to hide the smugness I felt, but her expression revealed that I had failed.

"Let me see!" Selene attempted to grab the box out of my hands.

I dodged her grabby hands and walked into the tiny kitchen, setting the container on the counter. I pulled the little card off the front and offered it to her. **Adelaide** *was written clearly across the front of it.*

I arched a brow, "I told you." The need to punch her in the face was becoming nearly impossible to resist.

"I can't imagine who would send you breakfast. Especially with me as your dorm mate. No matter." She rolled her eyes, *"It's obviously out of pity, knowing you're bound to stay a Passive."* A wicked grin spread across her face.

I'd become familiar with the look and tried to step out of the way but didn't do it quickly enough. Selene pretended to stumble and poured her coffee all over me.

"What the hell?" I screeched as the hot liquid soaked through my shirt and burned my chest.

"Enjoy your breakfast. You'd better get changed before you're late for class." The bitch sashayed out the door with a massive smile on her face.

༄ ❧ ༄

Now, I was in a rush, trying to make it to my biology class. I finally turned down what I believed was the correct hallway.

Despite being here for a few weeks, I still felt lost. The place was *enormous*. I'd taken a tour when I first got to Emberhold, but I was notoriously bad with directions.

I glanced at my schedule that I held clutched in my hand to confirm I was on the right track. I hadn't been paying as much attention to my surroundings as I should have because I was planning my revenge on Selene... then I ran into a wall.

"Shit!" I cried as my ass hit the floor and my bag flew out of my hand.

A deep voice growled, "You really shouldn't use that kind of language."

I looked up, preparing to give this guy a piece of my mind; then I froze. My first thought was that I must have a concussion from the fall because I was seeing double.

"I don't know brother, there's something about such an innocent-looking girl speaking like a seasoned sailor that does it for me." A guy who was identical to the first grinned.

The twin who was the first to speak offered me his hand to help me up. When we touched, I felt a tingling run from my hand up my arm. I let go so quickly that I fell again, but before I hit the floor, the second guy grabbed my arm and kept me standing.

The tingling started again, but this time instead of resisting, I leaned into it. Was it possible that I'd just met two potentials? Was I Nexus?

"My name is Jesse. What's yours?" The grin had fallen from his face, replaced by a look of awe.

I blushed, "Adelaide Hawthorne."

He kissed the back of my hand, "It's a pleasure to meet you, Adelaide Hawthorne. Can we walk you to class?"

"Yes, please," I squeaked, my mama didn't raise no fool. These two men were stunning, and having their full attention on me was both nerve-wracking and addictive. They had black hair, long enough to grip, striking blue eyes, and muscles that I'm sure were the envy of many.

I wiped the corner of my mouth to make sure I didn't have any drool running down my chin.

The twin I ran into first smirked, "I'm John, and if you're done admiring us, I couldn't think of anything that would make me happier than escorting you to class."

He grabbed my hand in his, and Jesse took the other.

We began ambling down the hall, taking our time, none of us in a hurry. It felt like an electric current was running through all three of us, and the sensation was incredible. I had to be one of the luckiest women on earth at this moment.

Jesse stopped abruptly. "What class are you headed to?"

"Biology." I grinned, then started laughing. We were all so engrossed in how wonderful it felt being together, we'd forgotten that critical little detail of where we were going.

John looked sheepish, "We should've asked before we walked a hundred yards in the wrong direction."

"I probably should've told you, but I was a wee bit distracted by your muscles." I winked at John.

He looked stunned for a moment, as if he couldn't believe I'd admitted that, before throwing his head back and roaring with laughter.

Jesse's grin was so wide it took up his entire face. "If you can make a grump like him laugh like that, there's no doubt you're ours."

Now I was the one stunned. I knew it was true, but usually it was frowned upon to mention it before initiation.

"Come on woman, let's get that fine ass to class before we get ourselves into trouble." Jesse waggled his brows.

This man was going to be trouble, of that there was no doubt.

"You know biology is on the other side of the academy, right?" John asked, still smiling.

"Of course I knew that." I stuck my tongue out at him... I absolutely didn't know that.

"Sure you did," Jesse laughed and winked at me.

As we walked, they started sharing a little about themselves, and I did the same. Our conversation evolved into a question-and-answer session, and the two men revealed their distinct personalities through the questions they asked.

"Were you expecting to be Nexus?" John stared at me intently, daring me to deny what I was to them.

"Damn brother, you should start out asking something like: What's your favorite color?" Jesse smirked. "Ease into it. Have a little finesse."

"You mean like you did earlier?" John scowled in annoyance.

Jesse sniffed, "I was just stating a fact. You asked a question to which we both already have an answer."

John rolled his eyes. "Okay, Adelaide, what's your favorite color?"

"You stole my question! I demand you retract it immediately!" Jesse dropped my hand and squared up with his brother.

"You literally just told me to ask that!" John said, irritation lacing through his words.

"I said for you to ask something *like* it. Not that same exact question." Jesse scowled.

Was he truly pissed off? I was trying really hard to keep the grin off my face. These two were going to keep me on my toes.

"Little brothers are a pain in the ass." John let out a breath in exasperation and shook his head in disgust.

"Just by a few minutes, asshole." Jesse poked John in the chest.

Shit, maybe he was serious. If these two decided to go at it for real, I hope shirts get ripped off in the process.

The brothers stared at each other for several very uncomfortable minutes. At least for me... they didn't seem to be bothered by it.

John rolled his eyes. "I retract my question."

Jesse smiled and extended his hand. John grabbed it, and they shared a classic bro hug.

These two were just too cute for words.

I was startled when Jesse turned to me abruptly, "What's your favorite color?"

"Umm pink?" Was he serious? I grinned.

"Are you asking me or telling me?" The smartass smirked.

"Telling you." I poked him in the chest. The arrogance in these two was strong.

"So did you expect to be Nexus?" Jesse asked, with a twinkle in his eye.

I held both hands over my mouth to keep from laughing.

"Are you serious right now?" John scowled, not amused in the least.

"I said we needed to ease into the question, and that's what I did." The goofball smirked.

I couldn't contain my laughter any longer. These two were going to be trouble... *double trouble.*

CHAPTER 2
JESSE

Her laughter was the most beautiful thing I'd ever heard. I could see by the look on my brother's face that he felt the same.

Adelaide was petite, with long, beautiful, pale hair that reached her waist, and captivating amber eyes. Her figure was stunning. I tried to keep my gaze respectful, but it was a challenge.

What were the chances that we'd find our Nexus the very first year we were at Emberhold?

Neither of us expected to get lucky enough to be in the same Faction.

Truthfully, I'd thought we might both be Nexus. We were unusually strong for Passives. John and I had an affinity for animals that was unlike any I'd ever seen. (He for drawing them to him and me for imitating them.) I suspected that when we became Faction our ability would be related to that.

"Well, here's your class," John stated unnecessarily,

since we had stopped in front of a door that had Biology written in a plaque to the side.

I knew he was as hesitant to leave her side as I was. Maybe a trip to the office was necessary. We were all first-year students, so it shouldn't be too difficult to adjust our schedules to fit hers.

"I see that." She laughed, pointing at the large plaque.

I had to adjust myself. I loved a good smartass, and she obviously fit the bill.

John grinned mischievously, always quick with a comeback, "I wanted to be absolutely sure you knew. I didn't want you to get lost before opening the door."

Haha, my sense of direction isn't that bad," Adelaide glared, but I could see the smile she was trying to hide.

I thought I'd better jump in before the moron I shared a womb with really pissed her off. "Would you like to meet us for lunch?"

"I don't know... I might have other plans," Adelaide smiled mischievously.

"Cancel them. My brother wasn't really asking." John scowled.

I felt my blood heat at the thought of her meeting with other men who weren't her potentials. I wanted... no... I *needed* a commitment from her as soon as possible. If we could perform the ritual today, I'd do it, and I knew my brother felt the same.

"Be there or we'll come looking for you." I narrowed my eyes, prepared to argue with her.

I preferred to wait until after the ritual to show her the real me—the person who didn't want to let her out of my sight. The guy who would use any excuse necessary to stick to her like a barnacle. But if she wasn't going to make this easy, then I was ready to go hard.

And yes, I meant that in every form of the word.

She shocked me when she grinned, "Just keeping you on your toes. I'll see you both at lunch." Adelaide winked and then slipped inside the classroom before we could reply.

"That little brat," John growled, but didn't attempt to hide the smile spreading across his face.

"She really is, isn't she?" My smile mirrored the one gracing his face.

I would admit to being slightly disappointed... I really wanted to have an excuse to go hard.

Not that I wasn't already.

We both stood looking through the small window in the door, admiring Adelaide. Neither of us was ready to leave. We'd found our Nexus, and she was perfect for us.

How had I slept with all those other women? Thinking back now, I was appalled. None of them were anywhere near her level of perfection. I should have remained pure and untouched. On the other hand, she would benefit from my experience. Yep, that's how I would look at it... I was doing it for her.

John thumped me on the forehead, "What the fuck, bro?"

"I called your name twice. What are you thinking about so hard?" He eyed me with suspicion.

"That I should have remained pure for our girl." I frowned when he died laughing.

"That ship has sailed, brother. Let's just make sure she

benefits from the knowledge we've gained." He waggled his brows.

Great minds think alike.

"We should probably get to our class," John said, but made no move to do so.

"We probably should." I agreed. Also, not moving an inch. "...or we could wait here until her class is over and walk her to the next one."

"That's a better idea. She may have trouble finding it and need our help." His eyes never left the window. "Who's that guy staring at her?"

I peered into the classroom, "That's Rue Walters. He's brilliant. I have him in my advanced calculus class. The guy has already finished all the assignments for the semester. Apparently, he's some kind of prodigy even as a passive." I frowned in confusion and wondered aloud, "Why is he even taking this class? He's way too advanced for it."

"I think the way he's gazing at our girl might answer your question." John motioned at me to look back through the window.

I took another glance, and this time I noticed the adoration on his face. "Well, damn, I guess we weren't the first to meet her after all."

"Seems that way." John sighed, "I need to look deeper into his background and make sure he's a good fit for her."

I rolled my eyes. "He's going to be a great addition to any Faction. The guy is brilliant, and not only that, his family is even wealthier than Ubel Brummond's."

John was stunned and asked, "How have I never heard of him?"

"I hadn't either until he was in my class. After seeing how smart he was, I grew curious and started asking around."

"You mean after you discovered he was smarter than you?" My asshole brother smirked.

I flipped him off, "Maybe that was the reason, but at least it's coming in handy now. And to answer your question, he keeps to himself. He's very quiet and if my sources are correct, doesn't really like people."

"Watching him make his move should be interesting." John snickered.

I nodded in agreement, "I also heard that he's in high demand. Several powerful people are trying to push him in the direction of their precious children."

John glanced at me, "Looks like their efforts are going to be wasted. He's clearly enamored with Adelaide."

"Who could blame him?" I shrugged. I wasn't a hypocrite. I'd only met her less than an hour ago, and I didn't want to take my eyes off of her. I needed to ask the brainiac how he got his schedule changed. If he were a possible Faction brother, we might as well start working together now.

"He should be able to help get our schedules changed," John whispered to himself.

Twin power for the win.

Sometimes it felt like we were one person. I was so excited that we would be able to stay together. We fought often, but I couldn't imagine being without him; it would be like losing a limb.

Neither one of us spoke again, and soon Adelaide's class was dismissed. When she saw that we were still here, her mouth dropped open in shock. I had to adjust myself just thinking about how those plump lips would look stretched around my dick.

"What in the hell are you two still doing here?" She put both hands on her hips.

Could she be any cuter? I just wanted to pick her up and put her in my pocket.

We decided it would be best to wait and help you get to your next class." John put his arm around her shoulders and led her away from the door. "You know how terrible your sense of direction is."

Adalaide frowned, but before she could respond, we heard a deep voice asking, "Are these two bothering you?"

None of us had noticed Rue Walters' approach; it seemed he wasn't too happy with our presence.

"Hell no, we're not." John was offended by the question.

"Watch your language," Adalaide said, tongue in cheek.

John growled and pulled her closer, then kissed the top of her head. "I'd rather watch you."

Adalaide just laughed. "No, Rue. Everything's fine. These two bozos don't trust my sense of direction."

"That's not the only reason; we enjoy walking her to class." I gave him my most charming smile.

He frowned, "Do you even know what her next class is?"

Of course, our new Faction brother had to be a smart guy.

I tried to bluff my way through the question. "Of course. Do you?"

"Absolutely. And, since we both have the same class, I'll

walk her." He grabbed Adelaide's hand and tugged her away from John.

John was too shocked to react, and by the look on Adelaide's face, he wasn't the only one. Though if she responded to his touch the way she did ours, her shock wouldn't last long.

Just as I suspected, Rue was going to be involved in this as well. This Faction was going to be envied by many. Some well-to-do Aurathions were going to be very disappointed when this came to light.

CHAPTER 3
ADELAIDE

I looked at Rue in complete shock. When he grabbed my hand and pulled me away from John, the same tingling sensation I had felt with the twins overwhelmed me.

"We were here first, and from the way things seem to be headed, you'd better get ready to share." Jesse glanced between my face and the hand Rue was holding on to.

"I don't know what you're talking about." Rue started walking, pulling me with him at a fast pace; not in the least interested in anything they had to say.

"Now you're starting to piss me off." John grabbed my free hand.

Luckily, Rue let go of me immediately, or these ridiculously large men could have torn me apart.

I tended to be a little dramatic on occasion.

John gently placed me behind him and his brother, and they both squared up to Rue. He tried to go around them to grab my hand again, but they weren't budging.

"I don't like to fight, I'm more of a lover, but in this case, I'll make an exception," Jesse flexed his ridiculous muscles. "Just slow down and let's have a discussion."

Rue growled, clearly aggravated that John and Jesse weren't letting him get to me. He glowered at them both, and I could almost see the steam coming out of his ears. "There is nothing to discuss. Now unhand her immediately."

I wasn't a wilting flower, and these guys were starting to piss *me* off. I'd only let them manhandle me because I was still in shock after Rue had grabbed my hand, and it became clear he was a candidate for my Faction.

I'd noticed him in class… because what woman in her right mind wouldn't? The guy was brilliant and looked like an angel: golden blonde hair, blue eyes, and a dimple in each cheek. Most of the women and half the men spent most of our class period trying to get his attention.

It was all in vain because he seemed oblivious to it all. To be perfectly honest, I was amazed that he even knew who I was.

"Enough!" I stepped from behind the twins and stood in the middle of the three guys. "This is fucking ridiculous!"

"Language, Adelaide," John mumbled, seeming unable to help himself.

"What did you say?" I tilted my head up so I could look into his eyes, daring him to repeat that.

"Shut up, bro," Jesse said, out of the side of his mouth. "Now's not the time."

John frowned at his brother but didn't repeat himself. Smart man.

"This is what's going to happen... Rue is going to escort me to my next class since we're in it together." I narrowed my eyes at him when he aimed a smug expression at the twins, and he quickly dropped it. "After class, you two..." I nodded at John and Jesse, "...are going to get lunch, and we're going to find a spot by the lake to talk things over in private." I made eye contact with all three men. "Are we clear?"

There was considerable grumbling, but eventually everyone agreed.

"I'd just like to interject that I love a woman who takes charge." Jesse waggled his brows.

John rolled his eyes, then, to my surprise, bent down to kiss my cheek, "We'll have food waiting." He locked eyes with Rue, "You'd better pull your head out of your ass and come to terms with this situation, cause we're not going anywhere." And of then he added, "Don't take your eyes off her."

Really? I could probably kick their respective asses.

Before I could tell him exactly that, both guys turned and walked off. I heard Jesse mumble something about heading to the administration office to change their schedules.

Rue frowned briefly in their direction, then grabbed my hand and started toward our class once more—a bold move for someone who hadn't said two words to me before today.

When we entered, I headed toward my usual seat, but Rue stopped me and pointed to the desk next to his. I rolled my eyes but didn't argue.

At this point, I just wanted a moment of peace to

digest everything that had happened. Now that it had become clear I was destined to be Nexus, I needed a minute to come to terms with that.

"Why is Rue Walters sitting by *her?*" Beatrice, Selene's best friend, asked no one in particular.

The nights that she came over, I made myself scarce. Dealing with them both at the same time was exhausting. Selene was difficult on the best of days, but with Beatrice there, it was unbearable. Those two seemed determined to make sure I was as miserable as possible. I had a recurring fantasy where both girls lost their voices permanently, along with developing the largest hemorrhoid on record. Sometimes I changed it up with them losing their sight and being forced to navigate a room where the floor was covered in Legos.

A girl could dream.

The sounds that came out of Selene's room led me to believe they were a little more than friends. Selene had to be Nexus if they were Potentials. I couldn't see her allowing someone else to be the center of attention. It gave me chills just thinking about what kind of fucked up Faction they would have.

Rue didn't acknowledge that she'd even spoken.

I wasn't quite so noble, "Wow, your ability must be in asking random questions that nobody cares about."

Beatrice opened her mouth to let her usual stream of trash fall out, but before she could speak, Rue's deep voice carried across the room.

"We don't give attention to ones such as her." Rue scolded me and turned his attention back to the front.

Beatrice gasped in outrage, but at that moment, the professor walked in and began her lecture.

I heard exactly none of it. I couldn't keep my eyes off Rue and my thoughts from the twins. My stomach felt like a flock of butterflies had taken up residence, and I had no idea how I was going to eat lunch surrounded on three sides by such male perfection.

Rue tapped one long, elegant finger on my leg, then nodded toward the podium the professor was speaking from. I wanted to be mad about his bossiness, but if I was being honest with myself, it was kind of sexy. I tuned back into the lecture, deciding to let go of my worries for now. Lunch would be here soon enough, and we could hash it all out then.

～☖〜

Class finally ended, and Rue grabbed my hand once more. For a guy who hadn't acknowledged me before today, he sure was making up for it now.

Before we could leave the classroom, Beatrice stepped in front of us. She hissed at Rue, "Why are you holding her hand? You know, Selene's father and yours have become very close."

Rue didn't bother to answer. He trained that frosty gaze of his on her and raised one eyebrow. The guy could give a look that would freeze you in your tracks. I'd witnessed him directing that look at professors who caved under it.

I gave credit to Beatrice because she didn't flinch.

"Fine, have it your way," she shrugged. "You're going to regret your decision, then it'll be too late." She gave him an evil smirk and left the room.

I waited for him to comment on what she'd said. When it became apparent he wasn't going to, I broke the silence.

"What the hell did she mean by that?" I asked as we exited the building and headed toward the lake.

"I don't know, nor do I care." Rue settled his serious, frosty blue eyes on me, "And neither should you."

I frowned, "It's not going to keep me up at night, but I am curious."

He stared at me for a moment, then sighed, "My father has business dealings with Selene's father. She and Beatrice probably hoped that it would lead me to become part of her Faction."

I stopped walking, and he looked at me in question. "Wait, does that mean she already knows she's Nexus?"

"I'm sure she hopes so. Whether it's so or not, I don't know, nor do I care. Regardless, my father knows better than to speak for me. I'll choose my own destiny." He gave a tug on my hand, and we began walking again.

He apparently was a man of few words. I knew next to nothing about him, only what I'd observed in class. If I were to be completely honest with myself, I was a little intimidated—not just by him, but by all my Potentials. They were all incredibly good-looking, and I was just... me.

Not that I didn't have confidence; 'fake it till you make it' was my personal mantra. I may have doubts, but none of the Passives in this school would ever be aware of it.

Just a small amount of blood in the water would bring the sharks in droves.

When we approached the lake, the twins were sitting at a table loaded with food. I was impressed because it was next to impossible to nab one in such a prime location.

Jesse got up and approached us with a smile that lit up his face. "I thought I'd exaggerated your beauty in my mind. If anything, I'd downplayed it."

He was quite the bullshitter; I was here for it.

Rue stepped partially in front of me, then mumbled to himself and moved aside.

Jesse gave him a small smile, then turned his full attention on me. "Come, my little cumquat, and see what delights await you."

"No... that doesn't work for me." I frowned at him. "No one as short as I am should have a nickname like that."

"Hmm, maybe you're right." He sat me at the table, then took the seat beside me. "Pocket princess?"

John took the seat across from me, and Rue sat on my other side.

"That's a ridiculous nickname." Rue sniffed as he filled a plate for himself.

What do you know about nicknames, Frosty?" Jesse stuck his tongue out at him.

Rue looked confused, "Who's Frosty?"

John started laughing, "I think he's talking about you."

"Me?" Rue's eyes widened. "Are you trying to give me a nickname too?" Rue's tone was highly indignant.

"I thought it might be fun since we're going to be

Faction," Jesse spoke around a mouthful of food. "Nicknames show affection. You should be honored."

Rue eyed him in disgust, then looked at me, "Are you certain he's a Potential?"

"Hey!" Jesse frowned at Rue, "Don't be like that. I bring a lot to a Faction, Frosty."

"Like what?" Rue squinted, still obviously annoyed by the nickname.

"Like me, for one." John grinned.

Jesse laughed, "Can't argue with that, Frosty. He's pretty great and *still* comes in second to me." He fluttered his lashes. "I have a fantastic sense of humor, I'm smart, well-spoken, handsome... shall I go on?"

"Lacks confidence," Rue commented, tongue in cheek, and tried to hide his grin at Jesse's overinflated ego.

But I saw it. Maybe these men could make this work in due time.

John rolled his eyes, apparently deciding a change of subject was in order: "So Adelaide, how prepared are you for initiation?"

I nibbled at the sandwich that Jesse had put on my plate. "I've been preparing for it for years."

"That doesn't really answer my question." He frowned, "What have you trained in?"

"I told you to ease into these kinds of subjects." Jesse slapped John's hand when he reached for a grape. "Those are for Pookie Poo, Bro. Keep your grubby paws off."

"No." I gave him a droll look.

He motioned, crumpling up a piece of paper and throwing it over his shoulder, "On to the next."

"She's been trained in all of the fighting methods

taught on Aurathia and a few from Earth. Also, she's had extensive training in survival methods and carries a pack with her at all times with supplies." Rue, aka Frosty, dropped all of that info like it was no big deal.

I looked down at the bright pink pack at my feet, then eyed Frosty with suspicion. What the hell?

"Damn, dude, stalker much?" Jesse asked in shock. He turned to John, "Is it wrong that I'm sort of impressed?"

Rue gave Jesse a smug look, "I take care of the things that are important to me." Then he resumed eating like none of this was out of the ordinary.

"How do you have all of that information?" I asked him, way more calmly than I felt. The fact that I was unaware of this level of observation freaked me out.

I needed to be better than that.

Frosty (I liked that nickname for him.) finished chewing his food and then wiped his mouth on a napkin. "You probably don't remember, but we've met before."

I wrinkled my brow, "When?"

"We were just small children and were both at the same birthday party...one of the Council members' children, as I recall. You walked by, and our hands brushed. I knew then our destiny was intertwined." He turned and began eating again.

"But how do you know so much about me?" I wasn't just going to let this drop.

He sighed and turned to me once again, "It wasn't hard, I did my due diligence. I needed to make sure you were being prepared properly, and you were. I've kept an eye on you since you arrived here, and it's clear that the fates saw fit to give me a Nexus that was superior to any other."

"Wow." Jesse said in wide-eyed amazement, "Just W-O-W."

John cleared his throat, "Well, as interesting as that is, I think there are other topics we need to cover."

I could tell John was going to be our mediator if this Faction ever became a reality. I, on the other hand, was still trying to wrap my head around Frosty's admissions. This guy was next level. I could see why so many Aurathions wanted him as a potential.

Jesse waggled his brows, "Sexy times?"

John hit him on the back of the head, "No, moron."

Frosty's face turned red, and he scowled at Jesse. "You're ridiculous."

I threw my head back and laughed. We were all going to get along just fine.

CHAPTER 4
SLY

I watched all four of them eat their meal, laughing and talking. I wanted to walk up and introduce myself, but now wasn't the time. It would happen soon, but timing was everything.

The very first day at Emberhold, I'd seen Adalaide walking across the quad, and I'd stood frozen in shock. It wasn't just her beauty that drew me in. She had an aura about her that drew the eyes of everyone in her sphere. Touch was usually required to affirm you were a Potential. It wasn't necessary in my case; I knew she was meant to be my Nexus.

There wasn't a single doubt in my mind.

"Hello... can you hear me?" Randell waved his hand in front of my face. "Is the air too thin way up there? Are you in danger of passing out?"

Randell was a close friend I'd known since grade school. He was a smooth talker with high hopes of gaining a seat on the Council. With his looks and confidence, I believed he had a good shot at achieving it.

"Sorry, what were you saying?" I ran a hand through my hair. My angel could distract me from anything and everything going on around me.

"Apparently, nothing that interests you." He smiled, not offended in the least at my lack of attention. "It would be hard to compete with Adelaide Hawthorne." He stared in her direction, "She's absolutely gorgeous."

I slowly turned my head to look at him.

"Whoa…big guy, what did I say wrong?" Randell held out his hands in defense.

"Are you interested in her?" I scowled. I had to accept Potentials, but I knew Randell had two of his own. He was probably Nexus, so he shouldn't be looking at mine.

"No!" Randell said nervously, "I was just stating a fact."

"Have you told anyone?" I narrowed my eyes.

"Told anyone what?" He questioned, "I just noticed that you were staring in her direction. Is there something to tell?"

"There's nothing to tell. I was zoned out thinking about the game this weekend, and I happened to be looking in that direction." I stared into his eyes, daring him to disagree with me.

It turned out that Randell was as intelligent as I always thought he was.

"That makes sense—nothing's happening with Adelaide," he said as he stood and collected his trash. "About the game, we should head inside now. Practice begins in a few minutes."

I nodded my head. I knew he was humoring me; I had

to get better at hiding my fascination with Adelaide... at least until I was ready to stake my claim.

"Hey, Sly, are you coming?" Randell called as he threw away the wrapping for his burger and headed to practice.

"Yes, just give me a minute." I wanted just a little more time. I was watching the actual forming of my Faction, and that was more important to me than anything else. With Randell gone, I could stare to my heart's content.

"Okay, man, but you know Coach doesn't appreciate tardiness," Randell yelled as he jogged off.

I knew he was right, but at that moment, I didn't care. I'd only joined the team because the coach wouldn't leave me alone. He'd started recruiting me before I'd even set foot in Emberhold Academy. I didn't think being late to one practice was going to get me kicked off the team.

Adelaide looked astounded by something Rue said. Knowing him, it could be anything. He wasn't very good at social interactions, but that might be the only thing he struggled with. The guy was a genius and had been watching my angel for quite some time. I hadn't interfered because he was sought after by every family that thought their child might be Nexus. He would be the perfect addition to the Faction I was hoping to build with Adelaide. It didn't surprise me that he saw the greatness in her, just like I did.

Now the twins were a different breed than Rue. I didn't know how they met her. It must have been recently, because I'd never seen them around her before today. They were both popular among their peers. I'm sure their good looks had a lot to do with that. Jesse and John were much sought after by all the Aurathions on campus.

Jesse was somewhat of a womanizer, but John was more selective about who he spent time with. Jesse was outgoing, while John appeared to be much more of an introvert. Both men were incredibly smart; I thought of them as the Yin-Yang twins in my mind.

They were both suitable matches for Adelaide.

If they hadn't been, I would put a stop to this ASAP, Potentials or not. My angel's safety came first, and no subpar Aurathions were allowed to jeopardize that.

Their personal lives aside, I'd never heard a bad thing about either man. They were protective of each other, and that would carry over to anyone they cared about. John was brutally honest. Sometimes that pissed people off. I appreciated that in a man, so it wasn't a deal breaker for me.

I tried to gather as much information as I could on all the Passives from our year and the year before, since I realized that Adelaide was mine. I knew she would be collecting Passives for her Faction—whether she knew it or not—and I wanted to make sure that all her Potentials were worth considering.

I wished with all my heart to be by her side during all of this, but I wanted to tweak the situation before introducing myself. I was a rough guy and didn't want to scare her away before I could show how beautiful we would be together. I had a lot to offer our Faction, and I wanted a chance to prove it.

I felt a hand caress my lower back. "Hey, babe, what are you doing just standing here staring into space?"

I winced, "Just going over some strategies we practiced yesterday." Frowning down at her, I continued, "You know we're not dating Selene, so I'd appreciate it if you dropped the 'babe' when you talk to me."

Damn! Selene was the last person I needed to notice my fascination with Adelaide. She was one crazy bitch and had been after me for years. I had zero interest because I knew just how evil she was. Other people may be fooled by her beauty, but I knew the outside didn't always reflect what was inside.

We had absolutely no relationship at all, but she didn't see it that way. I definitely wasn't her "Babe".

"My poor, grouchy Sly. You have too much on your plate; Kicking ass right and left out on the field. I could help you with all of that stress." Selene purred as she tried to nestle up to my chest.

I stepped back quickly and shrugged my shoulders, feeling queasy. "No, I'm good. If I couldn't handle it, then I'd quit. I'd better get to practice before coach blows a gasket." Her touch literally made me sick.

She pouted playfully, "Well, if you change your mind, I can get rid of my roommate. Beatrice and I would be more than happy to help you relax."

I shivered in revulsion at the thought, but she took it for want. That was one of the things I'd noticed when we'd first met. Selene only saw what she wanted to see. If she desired something or someone, she'd do whatever was needed to get it.

Selene giggled, "I see you like that idea. Just say when and I'll make it happen."

Much of her interest in me stemmed from the fame I'd gained because of my talent in the field. She enjoyed the idea of basking in my glory. Beatrice was fully on board;

she did whatever Selene wanted her to, no questions asked.

"It's never going to happen. I've got to run." I left so fast that there should have been skid marks.

"See you soon!" I heard her yell, not concerned in the least with me making it clear I wasn't interested.

The bitch was crazy, and her best friend was even worse. They were a big reason I hadn't made my move on Adelaide yet. Her having a room with Selene was unfortunate for both of us. I couldn't believe how shitty my luck was when I found out that little nugget of information.

I had no idea how to claim Adelaide without making her an even bigger target for Selene. I knew she was more than capable of dealing with her... as long as Selene fought fairly. But that was unlikely, and when you threw Beatrice into the mix, it scared me to death. Each of them was a dangerous, scheming bitch, who I suspected might be responsible for more than one Passive disappearing.

Both of their families were above reproach... but there were rumors.

Anyone who had remained Passive and had no hope of finding a Faction was considered lower than trash to some Aurathions. The shame of having these Passives as relatives was more than some could bear. The families of both girls fell into this category. Family members who were unfortunate enough to remain Passive seemed to take extended trips that they never returned from.

Selene and Beatrice were each dangerous in their own right...together, they were lethal.

As I headed toward the locker room to change my clothes, I knew that I had to resolve this sooner rather than later. The draw to Adelaide was beyond strong, and I was tired of resisting it.

The last sight of my Faction had them all laughing and eating. They were getting along like they'd known each other for years. Adelaide threw a grape at Jesse, and he caught it in his mouth.

I grinned. Soon... very soon I'd be right in the midst of them. Enjoying Adelaide's beautiful smile while my head was in her lap and she was feeding *me* grapes.

Get ready, sweet angel. We'll be together before you know it.

CHAPTER 5
ADELAIDE

About an hour later, we finished lunch. I parted ways with the guys and went to my next class, which was fitness and initiation preparedness —one of my favorites. Though they all tried to walk with me, I insisted I would meet them there.

Today had been a lot, and I needed a moment alone to get my head around everything that had happened. Each one of the beautiful men I was lucky enough to have as Potentials were more than I could have dreamed of. I looked forward to getting to know them better, but my Nexus status was throwing me for a loop.

We were planning to visit the Cimarron Forest next week to see if we were worthy of a Fellat bonding. This would help identify any Passives who were meant to be Nexus, and upon bonding, you'd receive your triquetra. The sacred mark that every Nexus was honored to obtain.

Even if a Passive was not bonded, it didn't automatically mean they weren't Nexus. Still, it indicated that the

Fellats didn't deem you worthy, so you would never receive your mark. The stigma that came with that scenario could be harsh.

This was a fate nobody desired.

I'd prepared myself for what could happen there, but I hadn't expected to meet three Potentials this soon, proving I was Nexus. I think what was freaking me out the most was that they didn't *just* feel like Potentials; they already felt like mine.

"Hey, Adelaide, wait up!"

I turned and saw Jasmin running towards me with a harassed look on her face, "Hey, Jas. What's going on?"

Jasmin had been my best friend since grade school. She approached me on the playground and started an argument over who liked the color pink more. I wore a pink jumper with glittery pink sneakers, and my hair was pulled back in a ponytail with a bright pink bow.

Jasmin had a pink dress with braids and pink ribbons woven through each. When we both noticed we had the same pink sneakers, she declared that we would be sisters in pink forever, and that was that.

"Damien cornered me again!" She panted, hands on her knees, trying to catch her breath.

"Why in the hell were you running? I know how you feel about him." I asked, confused, but grateful for the distraction from my thoughts.

Jasmin rolled her eyes, "Because a man likes a good chase! How many times do I have to tell you? When a man is as fine as my Damien, I can't just fall at his feet. He needs to work for it."

My best friend was quite the character. She and

Damien were clearly meant for each other. He'd gone to high school with us, and they had clicked immediately. The first time they locked eyes in the cafeteria, neither of them could look away. I think it lasted for at least five whole minutes, though Jasmin will deny it to this day.

Jasmin and Damien complemented each other in every way; both loved sports and were brilliant. He was tall and slim, built like a runner; she was only a few inches shorter and carried herself like a queen.

His mocha skin, pale brown eyes, and white hair were such a unique combination that he drew women like bees to honey. Jasmine wore her long, dark hair in braids that hung just above her waist and had hazel eyes that stood out against her beautiful caramel skin color. She drew the eye of every male in her vicinity.

Separate, they were beautiful, but together they were almost too gorgeous to be real. I couldn't imagine what their children would look like.

"What if he decides on a girl that doesn't make him work quite so hard?" I waited for the explosion. I knew my question would piss her off.

Jasmine didn't disappoint.

She threw her hands on her hips, "Then the son of a bitch isn't worth my time! I'd throw his ass back and find another more worthy of me."

I tried to hide my smile. She had decided from the beginning that Damien needed to earn her love. She was afraid that if she gave in too soon, he would lose interest.

Jasmine knew that's not how Aurathions worked. Damien was clearly a Potential, but Jasmine was nothing if not dramatic. And I was beginning to believe Damien had a bit of a drama queen inside him, too.

"The hell you say woman!" Jasmine jumped a foot in the air when Damien threw his arms around her from behind. "You know there isn't a man more worthy than me."

I threw my head back and laughed, "Looks like you've been caught."

Jasmine scowled, "You're supposed to be my friend. I can't wait until the shoe is on the other foot. I'm going to make sure to pay you back twice as bad."

I felt my face get hot, and I knew that I was blushing, so I turned and started walking. We'd known each other so long that she'd be able to tell by my expression that something was up. I needed to get away from her now.

"Oh no, you don't! I saw that look on your face. You'd better spill, right now." Jasmine ran to catch up, grabbed my shoulder, and spun me around.

"There's nothing to spill." I shrugged, trying my best to look innocent.

Damien laughed mischievously, "From what I saw, there's plenty to spill. Three tall glasses at least."

"You're an asshole." I scowled at the traitor.

"Hey, that's my man you're talking to," Jasmine frowned, pointing her finger at me.

"*Now* he's your man? I thought you were still running from him until he proved himself." I looked at her in disbelief.

"Not at the moment, but tomorrow is another day," she smirked. "Quit trying to distract me and spill."

Resistance was futile; she would keep it up until I told her everything. The most I could hope for would be to delay the inevitable.

"I'll tell you after class." I pleaded with my eyes for her to understand.

She stared at me for a few moments, then nodded. "Okay, but you're going to meet me for dinner and tell me every last detail of what happened."

"Absolutely." I sighed in relief.

"Why aren't you in class yet?" I heard a deep voice behind us ask, and I turned to see Frosty frowning at me.

"And just how is that any of your business?" Jasmine tossed her braids over her shoulder and scowled at him.

He looked at her in confusion, like he hadn't noticed the two people walking with me. "She's mine," Frosty stated in his no muss, no fuss tone of voice.

"Oh, this is going to be *good*." Damien rubbed his hands together in glee.

Jasmine narrowed her eyes at Frosty, then asked me, "Is this one of the tall glasses?"

I shrugged, "Maybe?" It definitely was, but damn, I just needed a moment.

"Girl, you definitely have some explaining to do." Jasmine turned to Frosty, "Just so we're clear, if she accepts you as Faction, you are *hers*, not the other way around." She raised her brow, "Don't make me have to tell you twice."

She motioned with two fingers, pointing from her eyes to his, "I'm watching you." Jasmine turned and pulled me into her arms, giving me a tight squeeze. "We'll talk later."

She whispered in my ear, then left with Damien to exit through the back doors.

I blew out a breath, "Frosty, why are you here? I told you I needed a minute."

"I gave you eight, isn't that a sufficient amount of time to catch your breath?" I wanted to be mad, but he looked bewildered by my anger.

"I guess it'll have to be," I sighed. There was no point in being angry with him. "Let's get to the maze." I put my arm through his as we pushed through the doors.

I stopped abruptly when I saw John and Jesse waiting at the bottom of the steps.

"You too?" I rolled my eyes. These men were utterly ridiculous.

Jesse laughed in amusement, "At least we waited out here. It looks like Frosty didn't even have the patience for that."

"I calculated the maximum amount of time someone would need to gather their thoughts. I then gave her an additional two minutes just in case my calculations were off." He smirked, "But I'm never wrong, so that was just an extra kindness. I'm known for that kind of thing."

All three of us just stood there with open mouths. Was he for real?

"It would be difficult to use mathematical equations to calculate how much time a person needs to regroup," John explained quietly.

"Maybe for you." Frosty snarked back.

"Maybe for anyone sane," Jesse mumbled under his breath.

"Come, Adelaide. Let's get to class. There are several

areas that I think could use improvement in your preparations for initiation." Frosty grabbed my hand and pulled me along.

I turned and gave the twins a pleading look, and they fell in behind us. Maybe Rue's nickname should have been Bossy pants instead of Frosty, because that's what he was.

CHAPTER 6
JOHN

We arrived at the Maze, as we affectionately called it, a vast field containing tall hedgerows going in every direction. They shifted regularly and formed courses we had to run.

There were various apparatuses scattered throughout the area, along with predators just waiting for you to slip up. Emberhold wanted us to be prepared for every situation that we might encounter during initiation.

We found a spot off to the side and began stretching. Some of the guys we'd been hanging out with paused to glance at us with curiosity when they saw us around Adelaide.

Neither of us was known to hang out with women long-term.

Most Passives slept around, hoping to get lucky and find Faction members. (It wasn't always as easy as a touch on the hand.) When it became clear that it wasn't going to happen, we tended to move on—no harm, no foul.

Now and then, we encountered a stage five clinger who didn't want to follow our rules. I didn't sugarcoat it when that happened, mainly because I made it clear from the start that, unless there was a connection, it was just a release.

My twin, on the other hand, tried to joke his way out of it to avoid hurting anyone's feelings. When that didn't work, he was willing to get a little more aggressive.

I personally didn't want to form an attachment to someone I'd have to give up when I found my Nexus. Others had tried, but in the end, those relationships never worked out. I couldn't imagine the jealousy and the heartache involved. In my opinion, it was better to wait.

A person might give up their abilities for love, but it was hard to fight destiny. We were hard-wired to want our Potentials, and that was that.

Jesse was eager to find our Faction and begin building a family, so he'd played around a lot more than I had. I liked my privacy and understood it could sometimes take years to locate a Nexus, if it happened at all.

I stared over at Adalaide in adoration.

Fortunately, we were among the lucky ones who didn't have to wait.

Jesse narrowed his eyes, "Move along. This Nexus is taken." When some of the Passives still lingered in shock, he bellowed again. "I know she's gorgeous, but she's ours… get your own."

My idiot brother managed to attract the attention of everyone within fifty yards and made Adelaide's face turn the color of a ripe tomato.

Adalaide paused in her stretching to give him a look,

"Really, asshole? There might have been some people over on the back forty that didn't hear you."

"What? I said you were gorgeous." Jesse said, completely clueless.

"He's a moron, but I promise he'll grow on you eventually." I rolled my eyes at my brother. Subtle, he was not.

"He's not a moron. I did my research after I determined you would be potential candidates for Adelaide's Faction." Frosty spoke but never paused his warm-up.

"How did you have enough time to do research? You only found out a couple of hours ago." Jesse stared at him in challenge.

"When you're as brilliant as I am, it doesn't take much time," Frosty said without any arrogance, simply stating it as a fact.

It was becoming apparent that he wasn't trying to be a dick. This was just who he was, take it or leave it. I could respect that since I also preferred the no bullshit approach.

Instructor Allen blew his whistle, and we all headed in his direction. I didn't let Adelaide out of my sight. I knew she'd made it this far without my help, but from this day forward, she'd have it whether she needed it or not. We hadn't even performed the ritual, and already my protective instincts were kicking in.

These last two weeks, I've taken it easy on you, as has Emberhold." The sudden gust of wind that blew in the wake of his words felt like confirmation from the academy. "Now it's time to step things up. You're going to be summoned for initiation soon, and I want to make sure more of you succeed than fail. Today we're going to run a new course. When I arrived early this morning, it was already set up and ready to go. I don't know what surprises Emberhold has prepared, but I'm sure each one is meant to help you get ready for what's coming."

There were sounds of distress coming from several different directions throughout the crowd. I looked toward Adelaide, but her face was impassive, not a flicker of nerves showing. I felt my chest swell in pride.

"Quiet! If this scares you, then chances are you're not going to make it through initiation. I wish I could say that upsets me, but the weak need to be picked off so our Factions won't be filled with pussys. Now line up!"

We stood and followed Adelaide as she made her way to the front of the line. I was going to offer to go first when, out of nowhere, Adelaide was pushed roughly from the side by a tall blonde.

"Let someone who actually has a chance of succeeding in this challenge go first. Our fellow Passives don't need to be discouraged by witnessing failure right out of the gate."

Another blonde, almost identical to the first, stepped up, "Selene's being kind, trying to save you from embarrassment." She sneered, "I'm not that nice, fuck off and let your betters go first."

I started toward the two bitches, but Frosty grabbed my arm to hold me back. "You have to let her fight her own battles, or she'll never be respected. Trust in Adelaide."

Jesse nodded in agreement, and I recognized the wisdom in his statement even though I didn't like it. I somehow managed to restrain myself from stepping in front of Adelaide and telling the two cunts just what I thought of them.

Adelaide smirked, not the least bit intimidated, "Well, if you're so sure I'll fail, why don't we make this interesting?"

"Hell, yes!" A beautiful, regal-looking woman standing behind us yelled, "Show those two bitches whose boss."

"That's Adelaide's best friend Jasmine," Frosty informed us.

Why was I not the least bit surprised he knew this? The guy had clearly been stalking Adelaide for some time.

"What did you have in mind, Hawthorne?" Instructor Allen asked.

"I was thinking we could do the course under time. That should make it a little more challenging. These two ladies shouldn't have a problem with that since they are so obviously superior to the rest of us." Adelaide smiled evilly, backing the two assholes into a corner.

Damn, this girl was perfect. I was so glad I hadn't interfered. My tiny Nexus was clearly a badass.

"I like it." Instructor Allen grinned, "Okay, girls, this is how it's going to go. Selene, you'll go first, followed by Beatrice, and then Adelaide will go last. I'll start your time as soon as you enter the course. Is there anyone else who'd like to participate?" He paused for a few seconds, "Looks like it's just you three."

Suddenly, there was a rustling noise, and the course started rearranging itself. I could hear big booms and sounds of scraping, and even a few mighty roars, but the hedges had grown so tall that none of us could see what awaited the girls.

The instructor let out a loud laugh, "Looks like Ember-hold is on board for this contest. By the sound of things, this course just grew exponentially harder." He rubbed his hands together, "Let's get this party started!"

I wholeheartedly believed in Adelaide, but that didn't stop a cold sweat from breaking out on my forehead. These courses weren't to be taken lightly... Aurathions died every year due to the difficulty they encountered when running them.

"Fuck this!" Jesse scowled, "No way am I going to allow this to happen!"

Frosty grabbed his arm, "You're not just going to allow it, you're going to put a smile on your face to show Adelaide how much you believe in her."

He frowned down at the hand holding him back. "I suggest you let go before you lose that hand."

I stepped in before things got out of hand, so to speak, "He's right."

Jesse turned to look at me, "Are you insane? He's *not* right! She could die in there!"

"She won't." Frosty let go of his arm. "I've seen what she can do. Do you really think that three strong Passives would be Potentials to a weakling? All three of us are strong enough to be Nexus on our own. Why would the Ancestors choose to give us to her?"

I raised a brow at Jesse.

"Okay, he has a point. But I want it on record that if one hair on her head gets damaged, I'm gutting both of you." He threatened in a low voice.

I nodded in agreement. If that happened, I'd gladly let him. I understood and agreed with everything Frosty had said; it didn't ease my nerves in the slightest about what she would be facing in the Maze. We'd be helpless here, unable to assist her at all.

I noticed Sly Iverson edging closer to Adelaide. He was hard to miss, being as large as he was. The guy was the star player on the Academy's combat squad team. The coach had tried to recruit Jesse and me, but we decided to wait until next year. Now that we'd found a tiny blonde Nexus who seemed to attract trouble, just like I'm sure Selene attracted venereal disease, I wasn't interested in joining at all.

He whispered something in her ear and walked quickly away. I think he was trying to go unnoticed, but I saw Beatrice nudge Selene then nod in Sly's direction. The look on her face at seeing the big man whispering to Adelaide chilled my blood.

That situation deserved some attention.

Selene started to move in his direction, but Instructor Allen blew his whistle. "Okay, Passive, let's get this horror show on the road. Get ready to go in five ... four... three ... two ... one!"

Selene scowled once more in Sly's direction, then took off like a shot, and soon she was behind the hedges and out of sight.

"It might be bad karma, but I hope the bitch gets eaten by whatever was making those awful sounds." Jesse scowled. "She's going to be trouble for Adelaide, and if something in there doesn't take her out, I'll be forced to do it."

"I second that. She deserves to have a bite taken out of her ass. Did anyone else notice Sly Iverson whisper something to our Nexus?" I asked distractedly as I watched Adelaide bend over and grab the back of her calves in a stretch that showcased her perfect ass.

"Yes, but it's not surprising since he watches her all the time. He's been sending her breakfast every morning from Java and Jam." Frosty's eyes followed the luscious curves of Adelaide's ass like mine did.

Seems like our Frosty wasn't always cold. It only took the sight of Adelaide's fine ass in worn leather pants to thaw him out.

"You didn't think that was important to mention?" Jesse asked, eyes also locked on Adelaide.

Three for three, all focused on one tiny woman's ass.

"I knew you'd find out soon enough. He's biding his time before he approaches her." He smiled slightly, "I give it to the end of the day."

I smirked, "Then there were four."

This Faction was going to be powerful. I had a feeling that after we performed the ritual, the abilities that each one of us gained were going to be unparalleled.

CHAPTER 7
ADELAIDE

M y nerves were trying to get the best of me, even though this was my idea.

I felt warm breath in my ear, "You've got this, Angel. Kick their ass."

I jerked my head up just in time to see Sly Iverson turn and head back into the crowd.

What in the world? Did Sly... *fine as hell...* Iverson whisper in my *freaking* ear? Sly was my favorite player on the combat squad team. In the last competition at the academy, he had single-handedly captured the other team's banner with only minor bloodshed. The guy was a celebrity here at Emberhold.

Jasmine and I even fangirled when it looked like he'd glanced our way at lunch the other day. Damien wasn't too happy about that until Jasmine insisted he was staring at me.

I thought she was full of shit- I hoped I was wrong.

Every female in our class fantasized that they were

either his Nexus or in his Faction. I was no different... the guy could crack bricks with his butt. Sly was close to seven feet of pure muscle, and I wanted to lick his abs, like a deranged Fellat with a bowl of cream.

Thinking about his warm breath in my ear made me shiver with desire.

I discreetly looked down at my chest to make sure my nipples weren't showing. That would be embarrassing. I didn't want to go through this course with nipple erections.

Whatever his reasons, his words had done the trick. I took a deep breath and centered myself. I could do this. I'd been training for years, and those two giant bitches could kiss my ass. It was time I put Selene in her place. Maybe then she'd move on and torture some other poor girl. Better yet, perhaps she'd quit being such an unnecessary asshole and stop making things more difficult for everyone.

I looked at my square-faced, hot pink timekeeper and saw that two minutes had gone by. I'd seen Selene run other courses, and I knew she was incredible. This wasn't going to be easy, but nothing worthwhile ever was. I knew what I could do, and I'd been holding back a little in class. There was no point in showing all of your cards straight out of the gate. You never knew when you needed to put a giant, blonde (my hair was a beautiful white blonde, theirs was a golden blonde...big difference.) shit-sucking, ass-licking, bitch that's breath smelled like an earring back in their place.

I glanced at Beatrice out of the corner of my eye. Now

it was time to play some head games. "Hey Beatrice, why do blondes like lightning?"

She looked confused at my question, "Why?"

"They think someone is taking their picture." I grinned.

Everyone started laughing, and Beatrice growled. "That's just stupid. You're blonde too!"

"Nope, my hair is a lighter shade of pale." I twirled my long ponytail around my finger. I was definitely a blonde, but that made it even funnier.

"You're an idiot." Beatrice snarled.

I wonder if she realized that rage-face made you wrinkle earlier.

"Why does it take longer to build a blonde snowman?"

"I'm not playing your stupid game!" She actually stomped her foot.

I heard a voice yell from the crowd, "Why?"

I recognized the sultry tones of my best friend's voice immediately. "Because you have to hollow out the head."

Everyone in the crowd started laughing again.

I glanced back at the time, five minutes in. Damn, this freaking course must be jacked. I glanced down at my supple black leather boots.

I really hoped my shoes weren't fucked for this.

Beatrice's squeal of rage jerked me out of my thoughts. "Everyone shut up!" Her face was now red with anger.

Just a little more, and her run would be destroyed. I knew I should feel bad, but really, I deserved an award for the shit I'd put up with. Both girls had been asking for this since I got here.

"How does a blonde's brain cell die?"

I waited because I knew Jasmine wouldn't let me down, but color me surprised when it was Frosty, John, and Jesse that screamed out collectively, "How?"

I paused for dramatic effect, then grinned at Beatrice, "Alone."

She screamed, then started in my direction, but stopped suddenly when Selene rolled out of the course, bleeding and covered in mud.

"Selene!" Beatrice screeched. Then ran to her side, "Are you okay?"

Selene rolled to her knees, then stood, "I'm fine." She looked at the instructor, "What's my time?"

"Ten minutes." He motioned for Beatrice to step up.

"Get it done." Selene growled, "I know you can't beat my time, but I expect you to come in close."

Beatrice nodded her head, "I won't let you down."

"Take your mark." Instructor Allen yelled at her.

He started his countdown, and I yelled out, "What did the blonde say when she found out she was pregnant?"

This time, the whole group shouted, "What!"

"I wonder if it's mine?" I screamed.

The timing was perfect because no sooner than the words left my mouth, Instructor Allen yelled, "Go!"

Instead of entering the course, Beatrice ran in my direction and threw a punch at my face that I easily ducked. She started to kick out with her leg, but Selene grabbed her by the arm and shoved her in the direction of the course. "Get your ass in there, time is running down!"

Beatrice shot one more hateful glare at me before racing into the Maze.

Selene scowled at me, "You'll pay for that shit!"

"No evil villain laugh to follow up that threat?" I taunted her. "Maybe some monologue?"

"Fuck off, Adelaide. I know where you sleep." She scowled at me.

After this, it was probably best if I requested a new room. I wouldn't get a wink of sleep having to watch out for those two psycho bitches. If I were denied, I'd sleep in the damn library.

"What the fuck did Sly say to you?" Selene demanded, staring at me fiercely.

"What business is it of yours?" I asked, feeling irrationally jealous at the thought of her knowing him.

"It's my business because I say it is. Now fucking tell me!" If she had the ability to shoot fire out of her eyes, I'd be dead now.

I couldn't let this bitch get into my head like I'd done with Beatrice. Focusing on the course was more important than bothering her, so I gave her an answer... not a truthful one, but she wouldn't know that.

"Good luck, that was all he said," I smirked.

"Stay away from him, he's mine," Selene growled out.

I just shrugged my shoulders. Until our Factions were formed, I wouldn't make that promise. I'd felt a certain type of way when he whispered in my ear, so whether or not he was hers might be up for debate.

Glancing down at the time, I saw that we'd passed the nine-minute mark. Beatrice wasn't going to beat Selene's time, but under ten minutes was still going to be tough to beat...at least for most Passives.

I had an edge over both of them.

I was smaller and incredibly fast. One of my fathers

was an extreme athlete, and I'd been training with him since I could walk. He'd never accepted the excuse of lacking abilities; he believed that Aurathions used that as a crutch and thought more Passives would be happier if they lived as if they might never be part of a Faction.

I watched the entrance to the course and concentrated on my breathing. I didn't know what awaited me, but I could handle anything.

If Selene could do it, I knew I could.

Finally, at twelve minutes, Beatrice limped out of the course, her left arm at an odd angle, clearly broken. Her mouth was bleeding… were those *teeth marks* on her leg?

Of course, Selene didn't show any concern and just motioned for me to step up. "Let's see what a *waste of space* like you can do."

Instructor Allen had summoned an Aurathion with healing abilities, and they took Beatrice to the infirmary.

Of course, Selene didn't go with her.

"I'll be sure to keep those three men you've been hanging around with satisfied. I'm sure they'd appreciate the attention of a *real* woman." She licked her lips and made a lewd gesture with her hips.

I flipped her off, "Maybe if they can get past the smell of your skanky ass vagina. I heard a rumor going around the academy that it smells like Parmesan cheese and bad decisions."

When Instructor Allen yelled Go, I entered the course with a smile on my face and the sound of Selene's outraged scream in my ears.

CHAPTER 8

ADELAIDE

When I cleared the hedges, I had zero visibility. There was a creepy fog that surrounded me, and the sounds coming out of it were enough to give me pause.

I took a deep breath, then jogged straight ahead.

Out of nowhere, a giant paw with ten-inch claws swiped for my face, but I tucked and rolled underneath it, then jumped back to my feet, already in a dead run.

What in all the Hells was that?! I shook it off. I didn't have time to dwell.

I knew the course made a giant circle, but the deeper in I got, the more a feeling of vastness confused my senses. I could hear grunts and growls from every direction, confusing me even further.

Stopping beneath the branches of a massive tree, I closed my eyes and focused. It seemed like I'd been here for hours, not minutes. Alright, time to woman up... I kept my eyes closed and relied on my other senses to decide which way to go.

Before I could come to a decision, a vine from the tree I was standing beneath grabbed me around the waist and yanked me off my feet. I gasped in surprise... what in the Little Shop of Horrors was this shit? I was lifted high into the air when I heard a groaning sound from below and saw the tree opening up, a giant, slimy tongue slithering out and up my leg. Rows of giant teeth lined the "mouth" that the tongue was pulling me toward.

"Fuck!" I yelled in absolute panic… then I remembered that I was a badass bitch that wasn't about to be taken out by a *damn tree*.

Pulling out the blade I keep inside my bra, I strained against the vine that had me in its clutches. With all of my strength, I leaned as far down as I could and sliced the tongue in half. The vine that still had me grasped around the waist started waving around frantically before sling-shotting my ass through the air at a rapid rate of speed.

My heart sailed into my throat right before I crashed into a giant hedge that somewhat broke my fall. I stood shakily, scratches covering my arms and a massive cut on my leg where the nasty tongue had been wrapped around it.

I shuddered in horror. It would be some time before I got over that incident.

I started to scan my surroundings, and I realized the tree must have knocked me most of the way through the course because I could see the exit. That was a small bit of good luck... I say small because I'd seen what was blocking the exit.

A giant, hairy Gerendel was standing directly between me and where I needed to go.

All of the Bigfoot myths on Earth stemmed from them and their penchant for wandering through portals. They weren't the brightest animals, but were absolutely vicious. Their teeth and claws could tear through flesh and bone like it was made out of papier-mache.

Think, Adelaide... think...what was my solution?

I tried to remember everything my Gramps had told me about the animals. I knew they had extremely poor eyesight but had an extraordinary sense of smell.

The thing was coming my way with its nose in the air. All of the blood that covered me was leading it right in my direction.

That gave me an idea!

I had one chance, and it had to work, because my time was running out.

I backed up slowly into the hedge. Taking my blade, I cut into the gash on my leg. Gritting my teeth around a scream, I squeezed it until there was a large puddle of blood on the ground. I then took my hand and smeared more on a few leaves that were on the backside of the hedge.

When I heard the beast coming closer, I waited as silently as I could, crouched low. When he stuck his head in, trying to find the source of the blood, I stabbed him directly in the scrotum with my knife.

The Gerendel fell to his knees and let out a sound that damn near punctured my eardrums. I would have felt bad, because a knife to the balls was awful, but they'd been known to carry off Aurathion children to eat, so fuck him.

I didn't waste any time and took off like a shot, sliding through the exit like a baseball player rounding home.

"Eight minutes!" I heard Instructor Allen yell, right before I was lifted into muscular arms.

"That's my badass girl!" Jesse tossed me into the air, then gave me a firm kiss. "I need you to promise me you won't do anything like that again without me. My heart can't handle the stress of you rushing into danger alone!"

"Put her the fuck down! She's bleeding, and we need to take her to the infirmary." John pulled me into his arms, then cradled me against his chest. "And you know she can't make that kind of promise, all of this shit is to get ready for initiation. Take reassurance in the fact that our girl kicked ass!"

I felt a hand softly tug my ponytail. When I looked over, I saw my Frosty smiling at me with approval. My chest swelled with pride as I grinned back at him. I knew he wasn't the type to give his approval unless you'd truly earned it.

The adrenaline I'd been high on left me suddenly, and I felt utterly exhausted. Right before my eyes drifted closed, I was almost certain I saw Sly Iverson in the crowd blowing me a kiss.

Shit, I most definitely had a concussion. The fact that he whispered encouragement before I ran the course was unbelievable enough. Blowing me a kiss? No way that happened.

⌁⚠⌁

When I opened my eyes, I was lying in a room in the infirmary with the lights dimmed. I felt renewed, and my leg was healed entirely, along with the cuts and scrapes from the killer tree.

"I'm glad to see those beautiful amber eyes open." Jesse, who was sitting on the edge of my bed, leaned over and kissed the end of my nose.

"Is our girl awake?" John walked into the room with three coffees.

The aroma was heavenly, "I hope one of those is for me?"

"Of course it is. Frosty told us how much you loved coffee." John set one of the cups on the bedside table.

"I don't usually approve of your caffeine consumption, but today I realize you could benefit from a boost." The man himself entered, holding a bag that emitted the most inviting smells.

"Tell me that's donuts from Java and Jam. And how did you get a fresh batch so late in the evening?" I held a hand to my chest, like the drama llama I was. Hmm, that could be why Jasmine and I got along so well.

Frosty smiled at me indulgently, "Would I go anywhere else? And I have my ways."

When he leaned down to hand me the bag, I pulled him in and brushed my lips over his - soft, testing - then began to lean back, breath shaky and eyes half-lidded. But his hand caught the nape of my neck, holding me there, and he deepened the kiss with quiet, unspoken hunger, stealing the breath from my lungs.

When he finally pulled back, it was only far enough to break the kiss, his breath hot against my parted lips. His hand still cradled my neck, thumb brushing my skin like he wasn't ready to let go. My chest rose against his with each unsteady breath, and for a heartbeat, neither of us moved – caught between restraint and the promise of more.

"That's enough. You need to rest." I could see from the heat in his eyes that pulling away had been the last thing he wanted to do.

"His nickname doesn't suit him *at all*," I said, still in a daze of desire.

Frosty chuckled darkly, "You'll soon find out just how true that is."

"Next time, I get to bring the donuts," Jesse grumbled, smoothing my hair back before handing me one of the heavenly treats.

Frosty smiled smugly, "Bring all you want, you'll never top my skills. I'm far superior to most Aurathions at everything, as I've repeatedly told you."

"Except modesty," John smirked.

Frosty shrugged his shoulders, "I've always thought modesty was only employed by those who were not confident in their skills."

"You would," John smirked. "How do you feel?" He shoved his brother out of the way and took a seat on my bed.

"I actually feel really good." I ate the donut in seconds, then made grabby hands for my coffee.

John picked it up but held it just out of my reach. "Frosty isn't the only one who wants a reward."

I smiled softly and barely had time to breathe his name before his hand cupped my jaw, and his mouth pressed against mine. There was nothing gentle about it—only heat and desperation, as if he'd been holding back for too long. When he finally pulled away, his breath was ragged, his forehead resting against mine, and I could still taste everything he hadn't said.

It felt like coming home.

When he leaned back, tears came to my eyes for some crazy reason. The stress from the day and the affection my guys were showing me were my undoing.

"What's wrong, my sweet girl?" John caught a tear on his finger and brought it to his mouth.

Seeing him take a part of me into his body made another bolt of desire move through me.

What were these men doing to me?

"Nothing?" It came out as more of a question than a statement.

"Are you sure?" He tugged a strand of my hair.

"I'm just so happy that I found you three." I grabbed his hand and squeezed it in mine. "Now hand me my coffee before I mess you up."

John smiled and handed me the cup. "Well, I'm sure I speak for all of us when I say that the feeling is mutual."

Just then, there was a knock on the door.

"Come in," John said in a cautious voice.

At the same time, each of my men positioned themselves between me and the door. The door swung open, and a nurse walked in.

"It's time for you young men to leave. Our patient needs rest," she said, walking over and taking the coffee out of my hand. "No stimulants. If you get a good night's sleep, you can leave first thing in the morning."

I scowled as she entered the bathroom and poured my coffee down the sink.

"We're going to stay with her and make sure she rests." Jesse inserted all of his considerable charm into his voice.

"Are you Faction?" Nurse Ratched asked, already knowing the answer.

"No, we're just first years, but we are her Potentials," John said, knowing where the woman was going with her question.

"I'm afraid that's not good enough. Only family or Faction is allowed to stay with a patient." She smirked.

"Those are the rules, but I'm sure exceptions can be made." Frosty stood and reached into his pocket.

The nurse frowned, "I know you're not suggesting bribery, Mr. Walters."

He pulled his hand out of his pocket, appearing more than a little frustrated. "Apparently not."

I'm sure he wasn't used to not getting his way, given his family's wealth and standing in the Aurathion community.

"Guys, I'll be fine. Get some sleep, and I'll see you in the morning."

I knew if I didn't speak up, they would get themselves into trouble. The academy had been known to dole out punishments itself; Anything from early initiation to making your dorm the size of a broom closet. I wasn't willing to see what it would do to the guys.

John stared at the nurse, looking like he wished he could melt her with his gaze.

Jesse and Frosty weren't any happier with the situation.

"Please, guys, I am feeling a bit sleepy." I needed to end this standoff before she called for reinforcements.

"Okay, but we'll be back first thing in the morning," John growled in the nurse's direction.

She just nodded, then opened the door and motioned them out.

Jesse blew me a kiss, Frosty and John followed suit, then left the room.

"I'll bring you some real food, then you need to rest." She frowned at my donuts. "And don't think those men can sneak back in here; I'll be watching." She gave me one more disapproving look before leaving the room.

I leaned back and closed my eyes. This day had been FUBAR, as my dads would say. Even though meeting the guys was a dream come true, I was looking forward to a new day. I understood it would get harder before it got easier. Right now, I just wanted to finish the initiation so I could do the ritual with my guys.

I drifted off to sleep with a smile on my face, thinking about those incredible kisses I'd gotten. Too bad, nurse cockblock, came in before Jesse got a turn.

CHAPTER 9
ADELAIDE

I woke abruptly when I felt someone lift my hands above my head, and I heard a soft click.

"What the hell?" I yelped in surprise.

"Did you think you could humiliate me and face no consequences?" Selene smirked evilly at the predicament I was in.

"I think she actually did," Beatrice said coyly.

I noticed that Beatrice had cuffed my wrists. She'd looped them around a bar extending from the wall behind my bed, used for IV bags.

"You better let me go, asshole. My nurse will be back here at any moment." I jerked against the cuffs to no avail.

"Who do you think snuck us in here?" Selene laughed, "She's a friend of my family."

Beatrice pulled a small knife from her pocket. "What should we do first?"

Selene slapped me so hard I felt my lip bust open. "I don't know; So many choices, so little time."

"That looked like fun." Beatrice dropped an elbow into my gut.

I was gasping for breath as Selene raised my bed, almost pulling my arms from their sockets.

"Now we have better access," She smiled in satisfaction right before punching me in the stomach.

Before the pain even had time to register, Beatrice followed her punch with another exactly in the same spot.

At that point, I'm sure my face was purple from the loss of oxygen, and I continued trying to draw in a breath, helpless to defend myself. I knew these two were assholes, but I hadn't recognized how truly evil they were.

I hope that oversight wasn't going to get me killed.

"Wait, I think she's trying to say something." Selene smirked, "Did you want to beg for mercy?"

I finally took in enough air to form words: "You hit… like a… bitch."

Selene scowled and then struck me so forcefully that I heard my nose crack and saw spots. I'd lied, she hit harder than should have been possible for a Passive with no Faction. But fuck if I'd admit that to her.

I felt something cold run across my face. When I regained my vision, I saw a knife glinting in the bedside light.

"I bet the guys won't be as interested in her if we scar her pretty face. Maybe take out one of those golden eyes." Beatrice smiled evilly as she gently stroked my face with the knife.

"We might not be able to get away with that, but shaving her hair would be an acceptable option," Selene smiled indulgently at Beatrice.

"But I wanted to see what she would look like without an eye." She pouted, "and you know what the sight of blood does to me."

Selene chuckled, "I know, sweet girl." She moved closer to Beatrice and gave her a long kiss that had both of them moaning in desire. "I never said I'd shave her head gently; that knife is sharp, so there will probably be some cuts and gashes along the way."

Beatrice giggled, "Let's do it together."

"Great idea. The couple that plays together, stays together." Selene laid her hand over Beatrice's on the knife handle and moved it in my direction.

I jerked and tugged on the cuffs, but I couldn't get loose. This was going to suck. As much as I abhorred giving them the satisfaction, I felt tears come to my eyes in frustration at my helplessness.

"Fuck you! You're cowards. You couldn't beat me in a fair fight, so you decided to prove just how chickenshit you are." I said, struggling to move away from the knife.

"You have me confused for someone who cares; It doesn't matter how I win, just as long as I do," Selene smirked.

"What the fuck is going on here?" Sly Iverson burst through the door.

A wave of relief washed over my entire body. I didn't know why he was in the infirmary, but I was grateful that he was.

"Sly! What are you doing here?" Selene jerked the knife behind her back.

"What the fuck are *you* doing here?" Sly walked over to

my bed, reached up, and crushed the cuffs with his massive hands.

I moaned as my arms dropped, and blood rushed back to them. Sly positioned himself between me and the girls. "Get the fuck out of here!"

"Why are you so worried about her?" Selene asked accusingly. "You're mine."

"I'm not yours… I'm *hers*." He reached back slightly and laid one of his large hands on my leg. "Now get the fuck out before I break your fucking neck."

Beatrice rolled her eyes and strolled out of the room.

Selene followed behind her but paused before leaving, "This isn't over, bitch. I told you to stay away from what's mine." She narrowed her eyes, "You should have listened."

"Fuck you, Selene." I struggled to rise and follow the bitch. I had no idea what I planned on doing, since I was pretty fucked up.

"Calm, Angel. She's not worth it." He turned and sat at my side, pulling me into his arms until I settled down.

"Why are you here?" I didn't even realize he knew who I was before today.

"I came right after practice to check on you. As to why, you heard what I told Selene. I'm yours." He gently lay beside me on the bed, then took my hand in his. "Can't you feel it?"

When I stilled, I noticed the tingling that began in my hand and then spread through the rest of my body.

"I do." I breathed. "How did you know? I know we've never touched before now." I smiled shyly, "I would've remembered if we had."

"The first time I saw you, I just knew." He dropped my

hand, then went into my bathroom, returning with a damp towel.

"Why didn't you say something before now?" I flinched as he cleaned the blood from my face. My lip was busted, and my jaw was killing me. Not to mention the terrible pain in my stomach.

He took a few moments to answer, "I've known Selene for years, and she's tried to claim me as hers for a very long time. I knew how dangerous she could be. I didn't want to bring her wrath down on you, especially when I found out you were roommates." Sly threw the rag on the bedside table and lay beside me, taking me gently in his arms once again.

"Did you ever have a relationship with her? Is that why she believes you're hers?" That thought made me grit my teeth. I probably shouldn't have asked, but I wanted... no, I *needed* to know.

"No, absolutely not." He drew me closer, "She's insignificant to me. Selene has spent years trying to change my mind, but I'm not stupid. She's only ever wanted me for my notoriety. Plus, I wanted to wait for my Ancestors' given Nexus," He grinned. "And I was rewarded for my patience when I saw you."

I closed my eyes and nestled closer to his massive chest, just breathing in his clean scent. He made me feel safe, and I needed that right now.

I sighed, "I'm not going to be able to let this stand. My pride won't allow it."

"I know. I wouldn't expect you to." Sly kissed the top of my head.

"There are three other potentials that I'd like you to

meet." I grinned up at him before my eyes drifted closed. I really needed sleep; this day just never seemed to end.

He laughed, "I've been watching. Each of them brings something unique to this Faction, and I approve."

I opened one eye, "Oh, you do, do you? I didn't know I needed your approval."

"You don't. But I'd think you'd want to stay on the good side of the man that's been delivering breakfast to your door."

"That was you?" I grinned, then winced at the stretch on my busted lip.

"That was me," Sly stood reluctantly. "Let's see if we can get someone in here to heal you."

"Will you come back?" I hated to sound so needy, but I didn't want to be alone. It wasn't because I was scared; it was because I didn't know if I could hold myself back from hunting those bitches down and kicking their ass. I knew this situation needed to be handled carefully, or I'd end up on the wrong side of the problem. I didn't underestimate Selene's intelligence or her connections... not anymore.

"Nothing could keep me away; I'll only be gone a minute." He smirked, "I know you can be impulsive, but please be patient. I'm going to send word to your other men, and we'll do some planning." He opened the door, then paused and glanced back at me. "My Nexus will get the revenge she deserves; I'll see to it."

Sly looked at me for a few more moments before he left, his eyes filled with adoration.

Had any Nexus ever been as lucky as me?

❧ ⚜ ☙

I'd fallen asleep soon after Sly left the room, but woke when I heard my door open. Apparently, I hadn't been sleeping very deeply because of the incident earlier.

Color me surprised when I saw all of my Potentials entering the room behind Sly.

Jesse rushed to my side, "What the actual fuck? I'll kill those two bitches for this."

Frosty reached my other side and scowled, "There definitely needs to be severe consequences dealt to them both."

John and Sly stood at the foot of my bed, a hand on each of my feet.

"There will be, but we need to be smart about it. The nurse who had us leave earlier is nowhere to be found, and it seems that none of the other staff have any idea who she was." John squeezed my foot gently.

I sat up, "What the hell? How did she get past everyone at the desk?"

Sly scowled, "I'd bet most of them were paid off. Her family is close to Ubel Brummond and has unlimited power thanks to that relationship." He sighed, "I'm afraid none of them would take kindly to you humiliating her in the Maze."

"Well, my family also has quite a bit of political power, and I won't stand for this." Rue leaned down and kissed the top of my head.

At that moment, another nurse walked in, but with a healer who followed close behind.

"What have you gotten into now, Ms. Hawthorne?" the healer asked, with a frown.

"Are you fucking serious right now?" Jesse growled.

The healer and the nurse winced as Sly snapped, "She didn't get into anything. Someone on your staff allowed Selene Tempest and Beatrice Sims into her room. As you can see, they thoroughly worked her over."

"I had no idea. I'm so sorry." The healer took a step back.

"You better believe there will be actions taken. After I inform my family of this atrocity to my potential Nexus, you'll be lucky if any of you keep your position here." Frosty clipped out.

"Sir, I have no idea how this happened, but you can be sure that we'll get to the bottom of it. Will you permit me to heal her?" he asked, timidly.

Frosty nodded his head curtly and stepped to the side.

The healer approached, but when the nurse made to follow, a low growl from Sly stopped her in her tracks. "Just the healer."

She nodded timidly, "Yes, Mr. Iverson. I'll step out of the room."

He didn't acknowledge her and turned back to watch the healer closely.

The healer closed his eyes and touched my forehead. Almost immediately, I felt my cuts and bruises healing along with the soreness in my stomach. All of my injuries would have healed in a day or so on their own, but none of my men seemed willing to wait, and I was thankful for that.

"Okay, Ms. Hawthorne, I believe with a little rest you'll

be as good as new." The healer said, stepping away from my side.

"If you think she's staying here one more minute, you're crazy." Jesse rubbed a hand through his hair, clearly aggravated.

"She's required to stay under our surveillance through the night in case she needs any more help." The healer wrung his hands nervously.

"Absolutely not. We'll be taking her with us, and if she needs anything more from you, I'll inform you myself." Frosty sniffed in disdain. "We've seen how safe she is here, and I won't stand for it."

Jesse cleared his throat.

Frosty rolled his eyes, "*We* won't stand for it."

The healer nodded his head and left, not having the balls to insist on my staying.

"Okay, Nexus, let's get you up and out of here. Frosty has the largest room and doesn't share with anyone, so we're all bunking with him for what's left of the night." John handed me a small bag I hadn't noticed until now, with a change of clothes.

When I looked at him in question, he sighed, "Frosty demanded the dean let us pack up your room. Although it's frowned on until after initiation and the ritual, he has also consented to let us move to Faction housing."

"I've never heard of such a thing." I gasped out in surprise.

"Neither has anyone else, but because of Sly's popularity and Frosty's family's influence, an exception has been made." John smirked, "Now get that beautiful ass out of bed and get dressed."

I complied, still stunned by his words but more than ready to leave.

After I changed, we all left, with Sly insisting on carrying me. I didn't put up a single protest. I wasn't a fool, after all; there were at least thirty Aurathions I could name offhand who would shank me to be in my position.

My best friend included.

We left the medical building and entered the tower where the first years were housed. Climbing to the very top, I wasn't surprised to see he was in the so-called penthouse suite, lacking a better description.

Emberhold obviously had a soft spot for his brilliance.

Frosty unlocked his door, then stood aside so Sly could enter with me. I gasped when I saw the luxury he lived in. My room was nice, but nothing like Frosty's. He even had a balcony I spotted through two large glass doors.

Before I could look my fill, Sly pushed through a door to the left of the giant stone fireplace. He passed a king-size bed, entered a large bathroom, and gently set me on my feet.

"Okay, Nexus, I'm going to run you a hot bath. Take your time, and we'll prepare you something to eat, then we'll all get some rest." Frosty followed in behind us and started running water into a large claw-foot tub.

These men had gone above and beyond for me. "Thank you, I really appreciate everything."

Jesse entered the room, "It's our privilege. Do you need any help undressing?" He waggled his brows.

"No, she does not." Frosty snapped as he poured bubble bath into the tub.

I frowned at him in disapproval, "I can answer for myself." I hugged Jesse, "I don't, but thanks for the offer."

Jesse stuck his tongue out at Frosty, "Okay, I'll head into the kitchen to help John."

Sly and Frosty followed behind him, the latter stopping to kiss the top of my head. "Yell if you need anything."

I nodded; when the door closed, I quickly took off my clothes and sighed as I sank into the hot water. I honestly didn't want to know how Frosty figured out my preferred bath water temperature.

Leaning my head back, all the events that had transpired began running through my head. Unfortunately, I wasn't lying when I told Sly that retribution would have to be served to Selene and Beatrice. There was no way I'd survive the academy letting that kind of transgression pass.

Lucky for me, I had four fine as fuck men willing to help me figure it all out.

CHAPTER 10

RUE

I was slightly uncomfortable having all of these people in my space, Faction brothers or not.

John had settled comfortably in my kitchen and was preparing omelets for everyone. He chopped an onion, a bell pepper, and a few jalapenos, then added them to the pan to sauté. Since I rarely buy food, I was surprised to see that there was anything to cook. I usually just ate in the dining hall.

"Don't look so surprised, I stopped by our dorm to get supplies," John smirked.

That cleared up that mystery. I sat at the bar, "So what are we thinking in terms of revenge?"

Jesse and Sly sat down, leaving an empty seat between them.

"I know what I want to do, but I'm guessing that's going to be out." Jesse dug into the omelet that John had set in front of him.

He slid plates in front of me and Sly, too. And I was aghast when my stomach growled at the delicious sight.

Jesse laughed, "It happens to the best of us. John makes a mean omelet."

John fixed a plate, stood opposite us, and began to eat. "I think we should let Adelaide decide. She's smart, and I have faith that she'll come up with something that fits the crime.

"I agree with John. Adelaide needs to be the one to come up with a plan. I'll support her in any way she wants, but it was she who Selene and Beatrice harmed." Sly spoke, not bothering to swallow his food first.

Disgusting.

"I also agree. In my observations, she is wise beyond her years, and I'm sure her solution will be acceptable." I dug eagerly into my omelet.

"We really need to talk about these stalking tendencies of yours." Jesse pointed at me with his fork.

Unlike Sly, I swallowed my food, then wiped the corner of my mouth with a napkin. "You've all benefited from my efforts, so I don't see the problem."

"That's the scariest part of all," Jesse smirked.

"Leave him alone. Adelaide doesn't seem to mind, so it's not our business." John rebuked his brother.

As I suspected, he was a man of intelligence.

"Whatever you say, big brother, but I reserve the right to revisit this at a later date. I didn't say I wanted him to stop; I want tips so I can become proficient in the future." He smirked and continued eating.

As I suspected, *he* was the *most* intelligent twin.

Adelaide entered the room, adorable in her pink

striped pajamas, with her beautiful pale hair in a wet, messy bun, and took the empty seat. John walked to the stove and started assembling her omelet.

"It smells delicious in here." She licked her lips adorably.

Everything she did was adorable in my book. When I realized she was my Nexus, I made sure to learn everything I could so I could excel in my role as Faction, just as I did with everything else.

My close friends and family might think that learning I was Faction instead of Nexus would disappoint me, but they would be wrong.

"It tastes delicious, too." Jesse finished his plate and had the gall to let out a huge belch.

I leaned away from him, "You're repulsive."

Adalaide started giggling, and at the sound, any anger I had drained away.

"He really is, but he's also kind of adorable, so I'll overlook it." Adelaide bumped him with her shoulder.

"I'm manly, and handsome, not adorable." Jesse leaned over and kissed her cheek.

John set an omelet in front of her, steaming and dripping with cheese.

We all watched in fascination as she took a bite and then licked the cheese from her fork, moaning the entire time.

I had to adjust my pants at the provocative sound. She was sexy no matter what she was doing, but seeing her enjoy her food was one of my favorite things. The sounds she made called to the part of me that loved a challenge. I wanted to know if I could make her repeat it with my head buried in her pussy.

From the looks of the rest of my Faction brothers, it seemed they were thinking the same thing.

"Damn, girl, I've never envied a fork in my life, but here we are." Jesse let out a breath.

"I'm with you, brother," John smirked.

Adelaide blushed, "Shut up, I'm starving."

"Leave my angel alone while she eats. We need to get our rest because we have a big move tomorrow." Sly finished his food, then brought our plates to the sink and began to wash them.

Well, it looked like the giant in our midst was civilized. Hopefully, the rest of them were house-trained as well. I had serious doubts about Jesse.

We cleaned our plates, then helped John finish cleaning the kitchen. Adelaide slipped into bed, and we took turns showering before joining her.

We played rock, paper, scissors to decide who slept where. I hated to admit it, but I actually enjoyed the rather ridiculous game. That was probably because I was one of the lucky ones who got to sleep beside Adelaide.

I was just as superior in this game as I was with most things.

"Are you okay with us sleeping here?" John asked, standing beside the bed.

"I wouldn't have it any other way." Adelaide scooted over, and he slipped in.

My bed was huge, but it wasn't quite large enough. It was a tight fit; we were all big men, especially with Sly's massive ass in the mix.

I heard a low, adorable snore (As previously mentioned, everything Adelaide did was adorable) and felt a level of contentment I'd never known.

This was everything.

As I'd mentioned before, all of my friends and family would assume that I would be disappointed at finding out I wasn't Nexus. The truth was, I'd never wanted that.

I got lost in my studies and experiments too often to want that title. I couldn't be happier with how things have turned out. I didn't want to be a Nexus with all the responsibility it brought. I knew I didn't have the emotional capacity for it. But I also knew it would take a remarkable woman to handle my long hours and how easily distracted I could become when working in my lab.

Not to mention the emotional distance I preferred to keep with the rest of the planet... except for my Adelaide, she was the exception to every one of my usual preferences.

The reason I was like this was simple.

I was exactly like my father.

His business and interest in council politics took up all his attention, unlike my love of science. My mothers had suffered from a lack of attention from him since their Faction was formed. It's truly a miracle that he paused in his work long enough to conceive me.

My father wasn't a bad man; he was just a terrible Nexus. He loved me and my mothers, that was never in doubt. But he was too self-absorbed to tend to his family.

Luckily, I hit the jackpot. Adelaide was beyond perfect, and even though my Faction brothers weren't, they were perfect for her.

As I lay here listening to each of my brothers join Adelaide in sleep, my mind drifted to my work in the lab. I was occupied with something that would improve the lives of all Aurathions. We've gone too long dependent on finding a Nexus to unlock our abilities, and I hoped to change that for future generations.

Finally, as I started to drift off, my last thought was that I hoped my Faction would be proud of my work. I was glad I'd found my Nexus, but many others wouldn't. If my work was successful, the world we lived in would become just a little brighter.

CHAPTER II
ADELAIDE

I woke up to the smell of bacon and an empty bed. I loved the first but wasn't crazy about the second.

I stretched, excited for everything this day was going to bring.

I'd considered what I wanted to do to exact my revenge against Selene and Beatrice. The choice I made wasn't as harsh as I'd prefer, but it would likely cause more pain than any physical harm.

Selene's pride meant more to her than anything else.

I rose and pulled on my leggings and an oversized sweatshirt. My pink bag was propped against the dresser, and I smiled at the sight. Frosty knew me so well, and in some ways, I appreciated his stalker tendencies.

I'd never admit that out loud.

I entered the kitchen, admiring this amazing dorm room. I hoped Frosty wasn't going to be disappointed, leaving all of this for our Faction housing.

I still couldn't believe that the dean was allowing us to move into Faction housing. None of us had been taken to initiation yet; to say this was unusual was putting it mildly.

Still, I was barely containing my elation.

"There's my angel," Sly smiled as he flipped bacon shirtless.

I almost swallowed my tongue. The man was F-I-R-E.

"You do know it's dangerous to fry bacon shirtless, right?"

That's the best you have, Adelaide? Was I encouraging the hot man to cover up all of those muscles?

I was an idiot.

"I think I'll survive." He smiled sardonically.

"Where are the others?" I swiped a piece of bacon off the platter it was draining on.

"That's going to cost you a kiss." Sly looked at me with heat in his eyes.

"I have no problem paying up." I fluttered my lashes.

Sly pulled me close, his bare chest pressed hot against me, and before I could catch a breath, his mouth claimed mine – fierce, demanding, relentless. My hands slid over the hard lines of muscle, desperate for more, anchoring myself against the heat of his skin. The kiss was all fire and hunger, my pulse racing as if I might burn up in the heat of him.

Suddenly, I was jerked away, and another set of lips took mine. This kiss was hard and consuming, leaving no room for air, no room for thought, cutting straight through me, sharp and unyielding, like he could brand me with nothing but the press of his lips.

When the kiss ended, I was in a daze, panties drenched in desire and unable to focus.

"There, that's better. I refuse to be the only one who hasn't kissed you at this point." Jesse puffed out his chest, seeing the condition I was in.

Sly smirked as he helped me to a stool at the bar. "Maybe, next time, wait until she's recovered from the kiss I gave her."

"Please, big guy, mine topped yours by leaps and bounds." Jesse teased as he grabbed a piece of bacon.

"Does he owe you a kiss, too?" I snarked, both of the guys just a little too pleased with themselves at my condition.

"Do I, big guy?" He puckered up and fluttered his lashes that were much longer than mine—the bastard.

"I'll pass on the kiss, but you can pay up by helping me take apart my bed," Sly smirked and fluttered his lashes back at Jesse.

"Your loss." The big goof grinned.

Frosty and John entered and joined me at the bar. "Where have you been?"

John gave me a peck on the lips and thanked Sly when he slid cups of coffee in front of us. "We went to confirm our housing and sign the paperwork involved."

"You should have woken me up. I'd have gone with you." I took a long sip out of my cup.

"No, you needed your rest. Have you decided what you're going to do about Selene and Beatrice?" Frosty asked, leaning in to give me a quick kiss, also.

Thank the Ancestors, both men had kept it short. I'd

never have survived two more passionate kisses without combusting.

"I have. It won't be as satisfying to me as beating their asses, but I think it'll be more devastating to Selene than anything physical I could do."

"Color me intrigued. What does this humiliation consist of?" Jesse opened the fridge and poured a glass of juice.

I narrowed my eyes. He may not be as perfect for me as I thought.

Catching my look, he started grinning, "I already had several cups of coffee before you got up."

Alright, I think I'll keep him.

'Well, I'm sure I still have access to our dorm room, and chances are, with me gone, Beatrice will be sleeping over." I couldn't contain my smirk. "Furthermore, I just happen to know an upperclassman who has the ability to create makeup that lasts for several months. Jasmine has used it, and her only complaint was not being able to wash it off so she could change up her look."

"I like where this is going." John smiled with pride, "A hit to Selene's pride is a completely brilliant idea."

"I told you our Nexus would come up with a fitting plan." Frosty shook his head, "How any of you could doubt my intellect at this point is astounding."

We snuck into the dorm with a satchel of makeup carried in Sly's arms. I'd asked for everything from fluorescent orange to pink glitter. I wasn't an animal; every woman deserved some pink in their life, whether they were evil or not.

Frosty had a substance in his lab that could cause them to fall into such a deep sleep that nothing we did would wake them up. All you had to do was uncap the vial, and it would release a gas that they would breathe in.

Thus, bringing about their downfall.

At least for a little while.

I pushed open the door to Selene's room cautiously, but they were both asleep—Selene in the bed and Beatrice on a pallet of blankets on the floor.

I shook my head in disgust. It didn't really surprise me, but I didn't understand how someone as beautiful as Beatrice could accept that kind of treatment.

I motioned for Frosty to open the vial, and I watched in awe as a purple gas floated directly to the women and surrounded them before disappearing as they breathed it in.

Frosty really was brilliant.

I approached the bed and used hand signals to ask Sly to help me turn them over.

"You know that you can speak now, so the signals aren't necessary," Frosty said, looking at me in confusion.

"I knew that. I just wanted to make sure you did." I gave him an innocent look.

He narrowed his eyes, "You know I can tell when you're lying."

"Or can you?" I fluttered my lashes.

"Enough of that, let's get to the fun stuff." Jesse rubbed his hands together.

John grabbed a jar of brown face paint and proceeded to cover Selene's entire face.

"That's a strange choice." I laughed.

"Nope, it's not. She wants to act like a shit, then that's what she'll be." He smiled evilly.

I giggled, "I couldn't have thought of a more fitting design."

"I'm so proud of you in this moment," Jesse said, kneeling over Beatrice, holding a jar of green paint.

"What are you planning to do with that?" John asked him.

"I was thinking of a witch, maybe I'll add a unibrow and a scruffy beard. Oh, and an eyepatch." Jesse said as he smoothed the green substance all over her face.

"I understand the unibrow, but what in the hell does an eyepatch and beard have to do with a witch theme?" Sly's face was filled with confusion.

Jesse just shrugged his shoulder, "I don't know, but it feels right."

Sly threw his head back in laughter and slapped Jesse on the back, "That's all that matters, brother."

After the guys were through with their designs, I sprinkled pink glitter all over their faces and poured the rest on Selene's bed.

Let's see the bitch get that cleaned up. She'd be covered in pink glitter the rest of the year.

You're welcome.

We took a couple of pictures to put on the walls of our new house... maybe in the bathroom.

Later that night, as we all lay in our oversized bed in our brand-new house, I couldn't have been happier.

Well, I could have, but after the last few days, we were all exhausted.

As I gently drifted off to sleep, I felt grateful to all the Ancestors for the wonderful gifts they'd given me. I was filled with hope and excitement about our bright future, eager to see what wonderful things lie ahead.

EPILOGUE

ADELAIDE

"One more push. That's it...breathe." Shannon said in a calming voice.

"I'm breathing!!" I growled. I knew I was being an asshole, but I found it hard to care in this moment.

Jesse wiped the sweat from my brow, "Come on, you can do this."

"One more push, Angel, and our baby will be here." John squeezed my hand.

I winced at being called angel but stayed silent. Both men had avoided that specific endearment since we'd lost Sly.

"One more push will do it." Shannon said, "As soon as the next contraction hits, give it all you've got."

I nodded. At this point, I barely had the energy to speak. It felt like I'd been in labor for days.

I felt another contraction building and bared down

with all my strength. I felt an intense stretching, then a gush of fluids as my baby slipped from my body.

Then silence... No crying, nothing—just complete and total silence.

"Is something wrong with my baby?" I screamed, jerking frantically at the guy's hands, trying to see what held them in a thrall.

My desperation must have finally reached Shannon because she brought the baby to me and laid it on my chest. When I looked down, I saw what had stunned everyone into silence.

The baby, my precious daughter, was glowing. Different symbols were appearing all over her tiny body and then disappearing just as quickly. Before I could even process what was happening, a symbol that shocked us all appeared on her forehead.

A scepter, the top of the staff, bore a Nexus mark emblazoned on it—something not seen in decades—with the length encircled by a black rose.

"That's the mark of Queen Lilibet!" Shannon gasped.

Everything Lee had told us had come true.

We watched in amazement as suddenly all the symbols faded, along with the glow that surrounded her. She looked like a normal baby, albeit a beautiful one.

I slowly raised my head and pierced Shannon with a look, "No one can know about this."

She was quiet for a moment, then nodded her head.

"I'm sorry, but I need a little more than that." I looked at John.

He glanced at Jesse, and they stepped up to Shannon.

Her face paled, "Please don't hurt me, I swear I won't tell anyone."

"I know you won't." They dragged her to the head of the bed, and I adjusted my baby, so she lay on the opposite side. "But I'm afraid I can't take the chance."

Shannon tried to struggle, but it didn't do her any good. I lay my free hand on her arm and closed my eyes.

My abilities had been weakening, especially this one, but the importance of this moment fueled my resolve. I felt my hand grow hot as I squeezed my eyes shut, sweat dotting my brow. After a moment, I noticed Shannon stop struggling.

"It's done, my love." John's words brought instant relief. Our daughter would be safe. "She won't be capable of saying anything now."

I looked over and saw Shannon asleep and breathing deeply.

"We'll take her home and find any files she might have been keeping. She'll never remember any of this." Jesse picked her up bridal style, and Shannon's head flopped back on his arm.

"I hated to do it, but it's for the best. Our baby's life could depend on it." I looked down at the precious bundle I was holding. Her head was covered in black fuzz, and she was staring at me with amber eyes that matched mine.

I felt a tear roll down my cheek at the sight of her. My sweet baby had a little of me and each of her fathers in her precious face. There was Frosty/ Rue's dimples; I hadn't even thought of his nickname in the longest time... it was too painful—Sly's pale skin, and John and Jesse's midnight hair.

I looked at John and Jesse, and they were both staring at her with reverence.

I had a thought, and I knew it was meant to be. "Her name is Reverie."

John and Jesse both nodded in agreement.

"It fits her perfectly." Jesse breathed.

"Yes, it does." John agreed. "Let's get Shannon home so we can get back. I don't want to leave you both alone for long."

Moxie chattered in irritation.

John laughed, "I know you'll keep them safe." He scratched behind the raccoon's ear. "But we don't want to be gone long, just the same."

I looked back at the beauty in my arms. She was my life now and a part of all of us. The only thing I had left of Sly and Rue. I'd kill anything that threatened her safety. Reverie was meant for great things, and it was our job to keep her safe so she could achieve that goal.

I had a feeling that the fate of Aurathions depended on it.

I kissed her little head, and for a moment, I could see Sly and Rue gazing down at both of us with love. "I vow that I'll do whatever it takes to keep our daughter safe."

Of course, there was no answer, but in my heart I knew they heard me.

ACKNOWLEDGMENTS

SURPRISE!

THIS one is for all the wonderful people who've read my books and given a new indie author a chance.

Thanks to everyone in my group, Frankie's Faction for all of your kind words and support.

THANK YOU, Adaira, Hayley, and Angie, for giving this one a quick once-over.

Also, I'd like to thank my wonderful proofreader, Trisha Elaine for getting this one finished so fast!

ALSO BY FRANKIE JAMES

Emberhold Academy Series:

Exordium

Inter

Exitus (pre-order)